To Nat.

First published in 2020 by Flying Eye Books, an imprint
of Nobrow Ltd. 27 Westgate Street, London E8 3RL

Text and Illustrations © Simona Ciraolo 2020.

Simona Ciraolo has asserted her right under the Copyright, Designs and
Patents Act, 1988, to be identified as the Author and Illustrator of this Work.

Published in the US by Nobrow (US) Inc.
Printed in Poland on FSC® certified paper.

1 3 5 7 9 10 8 6 4 2

FSC
www.fsc.org

MIX
Paper from
responsible sources
FSC® C001693

ISBN: 978-1-910620-95-3
www.flyingeyebooks.com

SiMONA CiRAOLO
SHY ONES

MAURICE ♥

FLYING EYE BOOKS
LONDON - NEW YORK

There's a new kid in town,
I don't know if you've noticed?

You may need to look twice;
he's not an easy one to spot.

He's not the type who stands out in class.

He's not the type who stands out in the playground either.

Unless you were looking for him,

you wouldn't know he's missing.

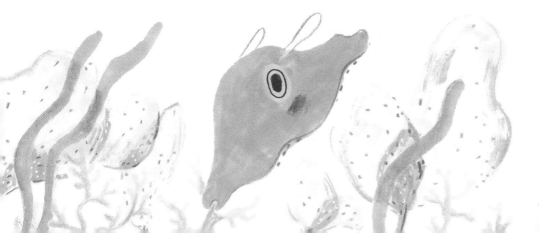

Right about now, you're probably thinking 'What a bore!'

But I wouldn't be so quick to jump to conclusions.

If only you had the chance to catch a glimpse
of him when he thinks no one is looking…

...you'd be amazed to discover the things he gets up to.

Oh, do invite him to your birthday party.

Perhaps he would rather not come, but he will make the effort.

He will be there, feeling a bit awkward.

How do I know all this?

You know us...

...the shy ones.

We always spot one another.